FRANKLIN and LUNA
and the BOOK of FAIRY TALES

JEN CAMPBELL • KATIE HARNETT

Thames & Hudson

Franklin and Luna love stories.
Stories full of ghosts and knights.

They read to each other when they're rowing on the pond,
imagining adventures with swords and magic wands.

Today is Franklin's birthday.
He's turning six hundred and six.

He's worried his friends have all forgotten –
they haven't sent him any gifts!

But, wait …
Luna's distracting Franklin
from all the people rushing by.

'Shhhh!'
Everyone in the village is planning a surprise!

Luna takes Franklin to a bookshop out of town.
It's owned by a lady in a velvet dressing gown.

It's full of spiders wearing spectacles
who organise the shelves.
There are books on every topic,
from art to magic spells.

It's the perfect place to spend an afternoon.
The shop is full to the brim.

Franklin can't believe his eyes,
some books are just as old as him!

In a cobwebbed corner by a grandfather clock,
there is a dusty book bound up in a lock.

Neil, Luna's pet tortoise, is a curious old chap.
He peers at it in wonder, not knowing it's a trap.

He breaks the lock when no one's looking,
ignoring all the signs …

… and when he opens up the cover, he disappears inside!

'We've got to save him!' Luna cries.
'Oh dear,' Franklin tuts.
'Going on a rescue mission
could be dangerous!'

They approach the book with caution,
it shakes and gleams and hums.

It whispers once upon a time.
It bellows FEE FI FO FUM.

They grab each other's hand
and without a backwards look …

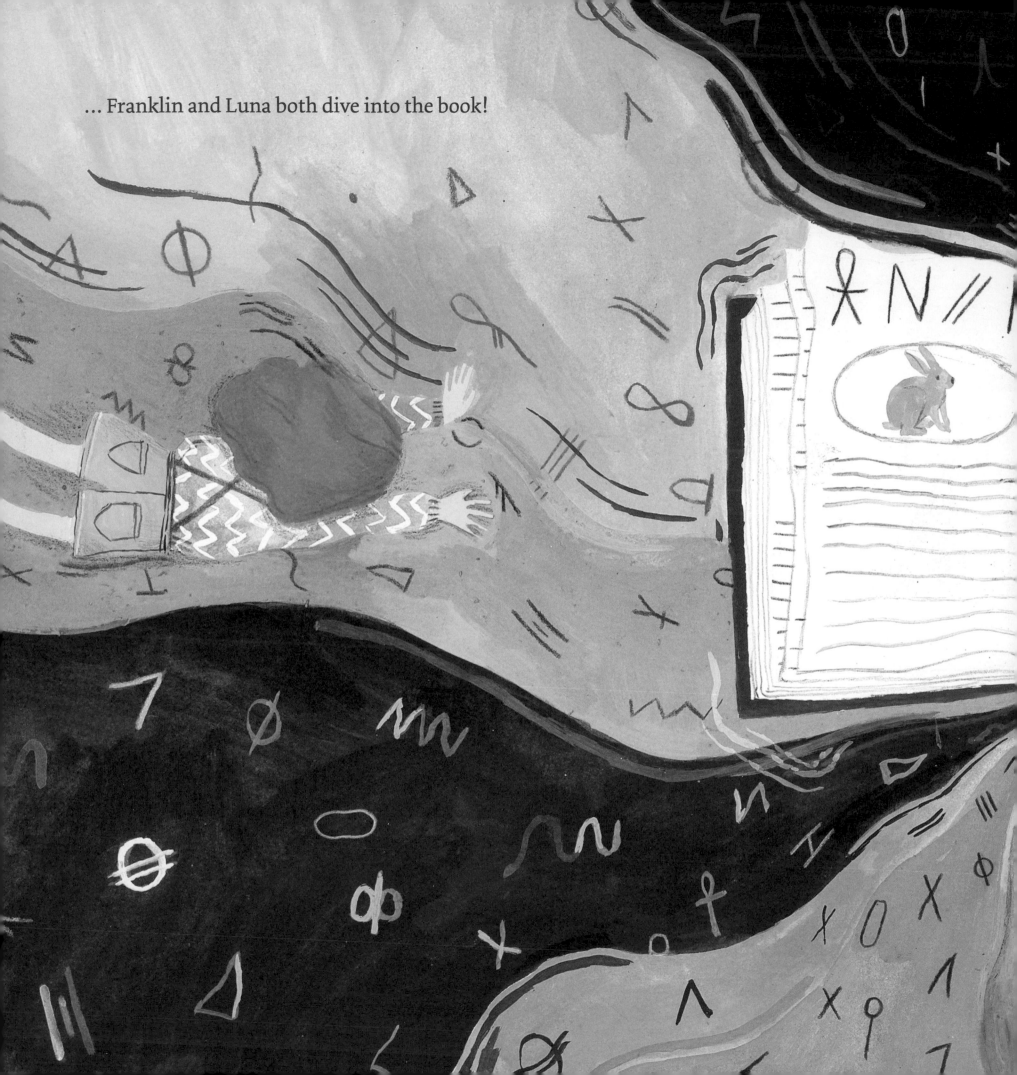

... Franklin and Luna both dive into the book!

They find themselves in a dark forest.
It smells of paper, ink and porridge.

'Neil, are you there?' they gulp.
They hear nothing back.

So Luna and Franklin set off along the path.

In a clearing, they find three little pigs building a hotel.

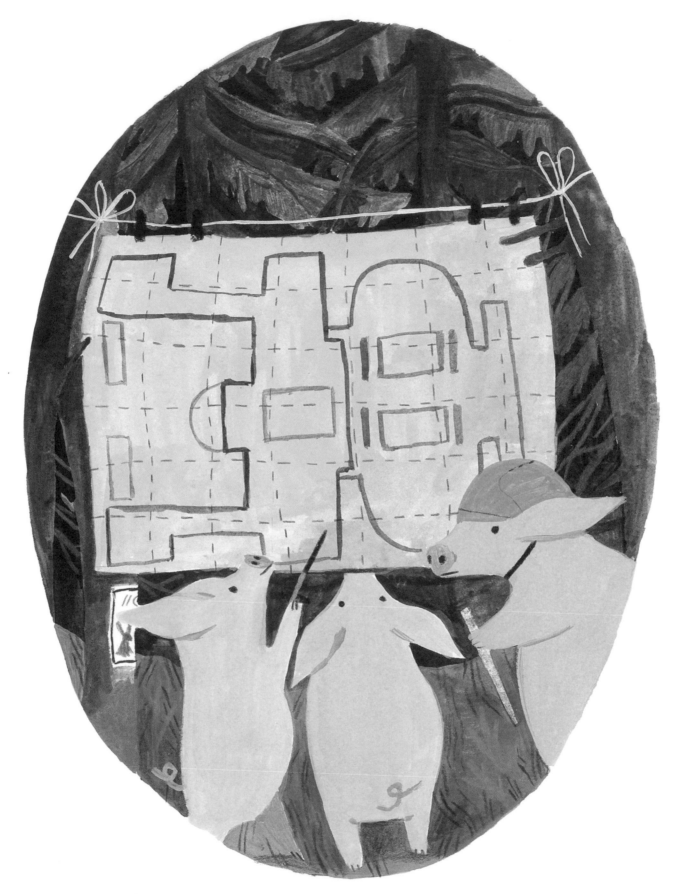

'Hello, there,' says Franklin. 'I hope you're all quite well.
Have you seen a tortoise? Did one pass by this way?'

'A tortoise?' snorts a little pig. 'In a fairy tale?'

'I don't think so,' says another. 'Not inside this book,
but if you're sure he's here somewhere, we can help you look.'

They decide to form a search party, calling out for Neil.
They meet three bears and a witch with a spinning wheel.

They greet a yawning princess with a bag of frozen peas,

and a boy who says he's sold his cow for several magic beans.

They find a knight inside a fortress.
'No, I haven't seen your tortoise.'

They pass a glass slipper shop ...

... then they see a flash of teeth and screech to a halt!

'Oh my, what big wings you have,' grins the wolf.
'Thanks,' says Franklin, looking pleased with himself.

'... Aren't you a bad guy?' Luna asks, unimpressed.
The wolf huffs and he grumbles. He puffs out his chest.

'You shouldn't believe all you read, you know,' he hastily explains.
'I'm vegetarian now. I do yoga, too. So, as you see, I've changed.'

'Did you say you're looking for a tortoise?' the wolf asks, his teeth bared.
'Because, if I'm not mistaken, there's one just over there.'

They find Neil the tortoise in a race with a hare!
'Neil, we've been so worried!' Franklin and Luna cry.

Everyone cheers loudly as he crosses the finish line.
'You were worried?' Neil giggles. 'I've been having the best time!'

Suddenly, the ground begins to tremble.
Their celebration turns to silence ...

... Running at them, footsteps thundering,
is a humongous giant!

'It's not me shaking the ground,' the giant booms.
'Someone's closing our book!
If you don't leave before it shuts,
you'll be trapped in here for good!'

'Can we come with you?' ask the little pigs.
'Us too, please!' they all yell.

'We want to see the real world!
We've got lots of tales to tell!'

They scramble on to Franklin's back.
He tells them all: 'Hold tight!'

The giant blows to create a wind
to help Franklin take flight.

The pages start to close
as they race to get away.

They burst out of The Book of Fairy Tales into the world again.

'Phewf!' Luna sighs, pulling everyone to their feet.
'I think we all deserve a rest. Come on, follow me!
Who would like a stardust scone or some lemon pie?'

'Franklin,' Luna winks. 'We've been planning a surprise!'

Franklin loves his party. It's a picnic in the sun!
He's so happy to celebrate his birthday with everyone.

Their new friends meet their old friends; they talk all afternoon.
Franklin's cousins have even come to visit from the moon!

'Is this our happily ever after?'
            asks Luna, drinking tea.
'I don't know,' Franklin grins.
            'But we have friends and books,
                and that's the best that it could be!'

'For Ollie and Phoebe' – Jen Campbell

'For my family' – Katie Harnett

First published in the United Kingdom in 2019 by Thames & Hudson Ltd,
181A High Holborn, London WC1V 7QX

Franklin and Luna and the Book of Fairy Tales © 2019 Thames & Hudson Ltd, London

Illustrations © 2019 Katie Harnett
Text © 2019 Jen Campbell

British Library Cataloguing-in-Publication Data
A catalogue record for this book is available from the British Library

ISBN 978-0-500-65175-9

Printed and bound in China through Asia Pacific Offset Ltd

To find out about all our publications, please visit **www.thamesandhudson.com**.
There you can subscribe to our e-newsletter, browse or download our
current catalogue, and buy any titles that are in print.